ONE WAS JOHNNY

by MAURICE SENDAK

ONE WAS JOHNNY

A COUNTING BOOK

SCHOLASTIC INC.

New York   Toronto   London   Auckland   Sydney

ISBN 0-590-45449-8

Copyright © 1962 by Maurice Sendak.
All rights reserved. Published by Scholastic Inc., 730 Broadway, New York, NY 10003, by arrangement with HarperCollins, Publishers.

12 11 10 9 8 7 6   5 6 7/9

Printed in the U.S.A.

First Scholastic printing, January 1992

FOR GENE

1 was Johnny who
lived by himself

2 was a rat who
jumped on his shelf

3 was a cat who
chased the rat

4 was a dog who
came in and sat

 was a turtle who
bit the dog's tail

6 was a monkey who brought in the mail

7 a blackbird pecked
poor Johnny's nose

8 was a tiger out
selling old clothes

9 was a robber who
took an old shoe

10 was a puzzle.
What should Johnny do?

He stood
on a chair
and said,
"Here's what I'll do—
I'll start
to count backwards

and when

I am through—

if this house

isn't empty

I'll eat

all of you!!!!"

 was the robber who
left looking pale

8 was the tiger who
chased him to jail

7 the blackbird flew
off to Havana

6 was the monkey who
stole a banana

5 was the turtle who
crawled off to bed

4 was the dog who
slid home on a sled

3 was the cat who
pounced on the rat

2 was the rat who
left with the cat

1 was Johnny who
lived by himself

AND LIKED IT LIKE THAT!